The AMAZING ADVENTURES of BATMAN ™

BANE DRAIN

by **Brandon T. Snider**
illustrated by **Dario Brizuela**

Batman created by Bob Kane with Bill Finger

PICTURE WINDOW BOOKS
a capstone imprint

Published by Picture Window Books, an imprint of Capstone.
1710 Roe Crest Drive
North Mankato, Minnesota 56003
www.capstonepub.com

Library of Congress Cataloging-in-Publication Data is available on the
Library of Congress website.
ISBN: 978-1-5158-4825-7 (library binding)
ISBN: 978-1-5158-5884-3 (paperback)
ISBN: 978-1-5158-4830-1 (eBook PDF)

Summary: Bane is on the loose at a Gotham City baseball game! An extra
dose of venom has made him stronger than ever. Can Batman and Batwing
drain Bane of his powers, or will the duo pull the plug on this case? Find out
in this action-packed early chapter book for the youngest of readers.

Designer: Kayla Rossow

Printed in the United States of America.
PA100

TABLE OF CONTENTS

Play Ball...................................7

Batter Up...............................13

Strike Out...........................19

Batman's Secret Message!............28

Hidden in the shadows,
a hero keeps watch.
He is the Caped Crusader
against crime. He is the
Dark Knight of justice.
These are ...

The AMAZING ADVENTURES of
BATMAN

CHAPTER 1

PLAY BALL

Crowds cheer inside Gotham City Stadium. Baseball fans celebrate a big win for their home team, the Gotham Knights.

Suddenly the stands shake beneath their feet. The stadium rumbles. **RUMMBBBBLE!**

BWOOOM!

The pitcher's mound explodes in a cloud of sand. When the dust clears, a masked man stands on the field. It's Bane!

Frightened fans run for safety.

Within minutes, Batman swings into the stadium on his Batrope. "Game over," the Dark Knight tells the villain.

"HA!" Bane laughs. "I'm just warming up! Before I'm through, the fans will be cheering for me."

Bane leaps into the stands.
The villain rips out a row of seats
and throws them at Batman.

Batman jumps up to avoid
the attack. *Time for me to call the
bull pen,* thinks the super hero.

BEEP! BEEP! BEEP!

Across town, Luke Fox answers his communication device. "What's going on, Batman?" Luke asks.

"Bane is on the loose at the Gotham City Stadium," Batman replies. "Looks like he wants to play hardball."

"Then let's knock him out of the park!" Luke says.

Moments later, the hero hops into his uniform. He soars into the sky. "Batwing to the rescue!"

CHAPTER 2

BATTER UP

Back at the stadium, Bane flexes his arms. "How about a game of catch?" he asks Batman.

Bane charges at Batman like a bull. He grabs the Dark Knight and lifts the hero high above his head.

"Put him down!" comes a voice from left field. It's Batwing!

"Make me," Bane growls.

"You asked for it," says Batwing.

PSHHH! The hero blasts Bane with sleeping gas. "It's lights out, big boy!" Batwing exclaims.

As Bane stumbles, Batman

escapes the villain's grasp.

He quickly joins his partner.

"Thanks, Batwing," says the

Dark Knight. "But that won't

keep Bane down for long."

"Then what's the game plan?"

Batwing asks.

Batman points to a thick, red
tube on the back of Bane's suit.
"That tube pumps toxic venom
into Bane's body. It's how he gets
his powers," the hero says. Then
he adds, "Cut the tube, and he's—"

"Outta here!" Batwing finishes.

Batwing rushes into battle

without thinking. Batman tries

to stop him, but it's too late.

Bane is itching for a fight.

"Batter up!" he snarls.

Just then, Bane fires up the

stadium's pitching machine.

THWOMP! THWOMP! THWOMP!

Baseballs hit Batwing so fast

that he falls to the ground.

"Uhn . . ." the hero moans.

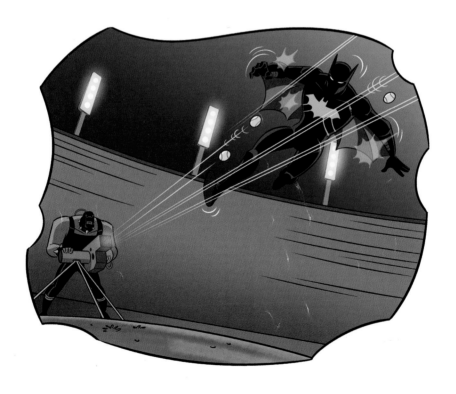

Chapter 3

STRIKE OUT

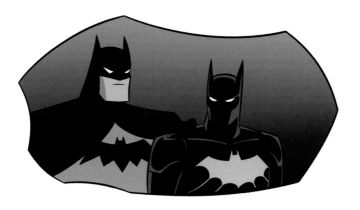

Batman rushes to Batwing's

side. "We have to work together,"

says the Dark Knight. "As a team."

"How do we stop Bane if we

can't get close?" Batwing asks.

Before Batman answers, Bane

corners a group of fleeing fans.

BOOM! BOOM! BOOM!

Bane pounds his fists into the ground. Frightened fans fly into the air. Batman and Batwing spring into action to save them.

FWOOSH! Batman swings to the rescue. He catches two fans before they hit the ground.

Batwing swoops and grabs a little girl. "Gotcha!" he exclaims.

With the fans safe, Batman and Batwing turn back to Bane.

The villain grabs a baseball bat from the nearby dugout. **KRAK!** He breaks the bat into two pieces.

"Next I will break you," the super-villain tells Batwing.

FWOOSH! Bane launches the pieces like missiles. Batwing catches them with ease.

Batwing strikes Bane. The two enemies battle back and forth.

Meanwhile, Batman grabs a Batarang from his Utility Belt and tosses it. The weapon slices the tube on Bane's costume. Venom sprays everywhere!

"STRIKKKKKE!" Batman calls.

"No!" Bane cries.

"Now, Batwing!" the Dark

Knight shouts.

Batwing grabs a baseball from a nearby bag. He winds up and throws it like an all-star pitcher.

CRACK! The baseball hits Bane square in the nose. "You're out!" Batwing says.

BOOM! Bane falls to the ground. The fans still inside the stadium cheer. "Batwing! Batwing! Batwing!" they shout.

"Thanks for another amazing adventure, Batwing," Batman says.

"Don't mention it," says his partner. "Glad I could step up to the plate."

BATMAN'S
SECRET MESSAGE!

What is the super-steroid that gives
Bane his powers called?

22 5 14 17 13

Use the code below to solve the
Batcomputer's secret message!

1	2	3	4	5	6	7	8	9	10	11	12	13
A	B	C	D	E	F	G	H	I	J	K	L	M

14	15	16	17	18	19	20	21	22	23	24	25	26
N	O	P	Q	R	S	T	U	V	W	X	Y	Z

bull pen (BUHL PEN)—a place on a baseball field where pitchers warm up before they start pitching

communication (kuh-MYOO-nuh-kay-shuhn)—a system for sending and receiving messages

flex (FLEKS)—to bend or stretch something, like muscles

stadium (STAY-dee-uhm)—a large building for sporting events, which contains a field and rows of seats

stumble (STUHM-buhl)—to trip, or walk in an unsteady way

toxic (TOK-sik)—another word for poisonous

villain (VIL-uhn)—a wicked, evil person

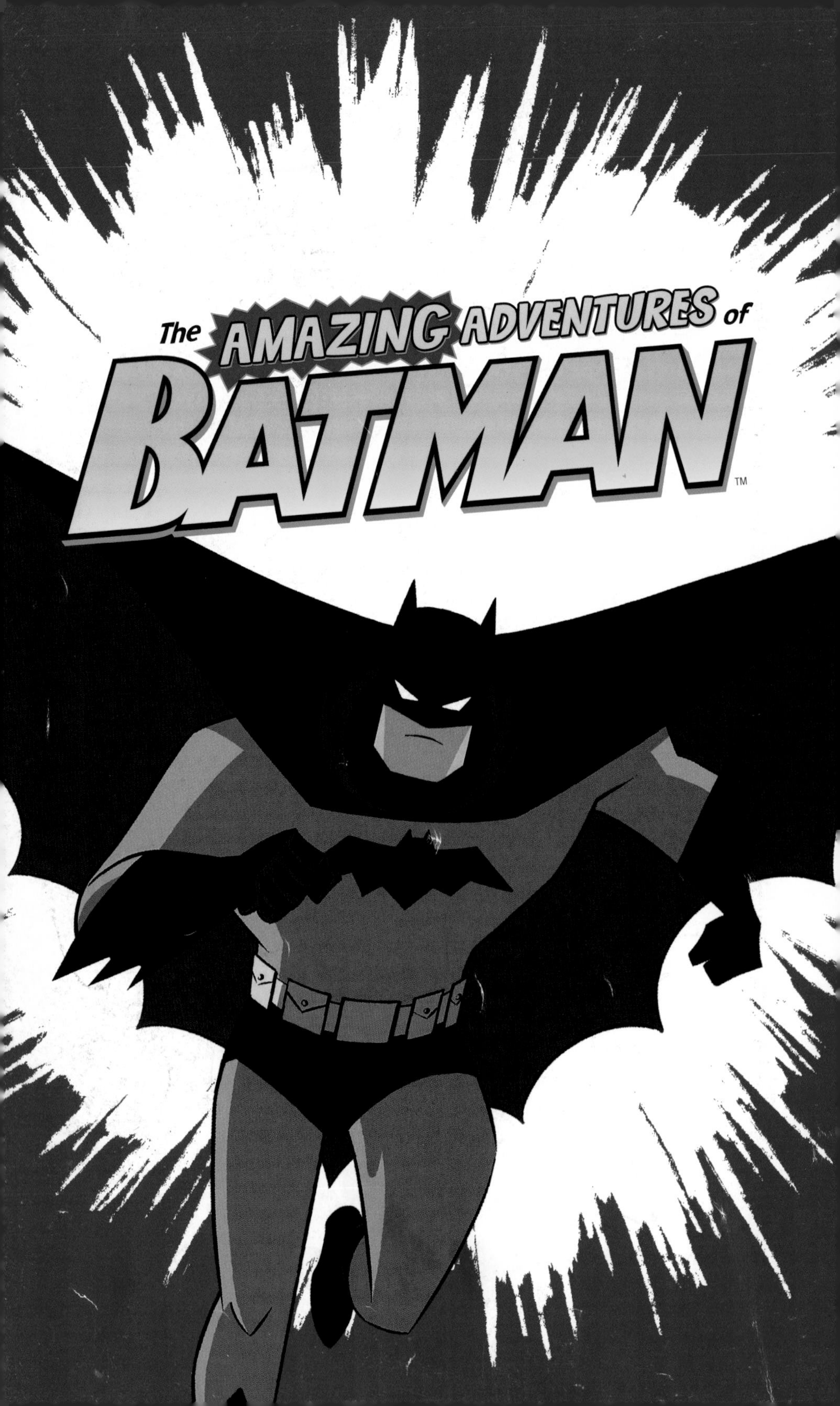
The AMAZING ADVENTURES of
BATMAN™

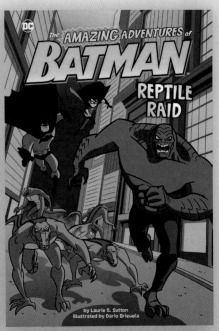

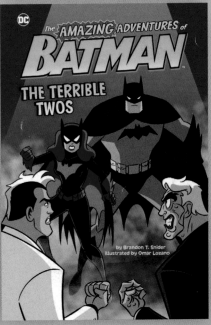

COLLECT THEM ALL!

only from . . . **PICTURE WINDOW BOOKS**

Author

Brandon T. Snider has authored over 50 books featuring pop culture icons such as Captain Kirk, Transformers and the Muppets. Additionally, he's written books for Cartoon Network favorites such as Adventure Time, Regular Show, and Powerpuff Girls. His award-winning *Dark Knight Manual* was mentioned in Entertainment Weekly, Forbes, and Wired. Brandon lives in New York City and is a member of the Writer's Guild of America.

Illustrator

Dario Brizuela was born in Buenos Aires, Argentina, and as a teen he began studying in an art school—doing drawing, sculpture, painting, and more. After discovering super hero comic books, his goal was draw his favorite characters. He broke into comics by working for publishers like Dark Horse Comics, Image, Mirage Studios, IDW, Titan Publishing, Soleil Productions, Viz Media, Little, Brown and Company, DC Comics, and Marvel Comics, and for companies like Hasbro and Lego. His comic book and illustration work in the U.S. and Europe includes: Star Wars Tales, Dioramas, Ben 10, Super Friends, Justice League Unlimited, Voltron Force, Batman: The Brave and the Bold, Transfomers, Mini Hulks, Gormiti, Superhero Squad, Scooby Doo, and Beware The Batman.